FINAL GIFT

MICHAEL WARREN LUCAS

Tilted Windmill Press

COPYRIGHT INFORMATION

ACKNOWLEDGEMENTS

My thanks go to all the Prohibition Orcs fans who demanded more. I promise you, more orc tales exist and you'll see them before long.

Special thanks to my Patronizers for financially supporting my career. Jeff Marracini, Kate Ebneter, Phil Vuchetich, and Stefan Johnson support me so much that I must list them in both the print and ebook editions of everything I do. My gratitude to you all.

1

When November's wind clawed at the plank walls of the old wooden barn where Mha lived, when it set the flames in the rusty coal stove of the grooms' quarters to flickering, when the hard-used joints between her ancient orcish bones swelled enough to make every motion torment, when her crumbling guts refused to release the giant turd-brick wedged inside, Mha couldn't help asking in the secret pit of her heart: why hadn't her children eaten her?

She already knew the answer, even on this bitterest of days.

Mha had borne two sons for her Uraz-n'Tass. One son died in the Great War; the other, crushed beneath a falling crane at the Port of Detroit. Other clans had claimed her three daughters.

They had done right by their children.

Even if it left them alone.

Even if a son had survived and kept the clan alive, she would still draw breath. This horrid America of 1927 left the old to rot alive.

And she and Uraz had rotted. Mha couldn't remember ever seeing an orc as old as them. Her beautiful bald purple-green scalp had sprouted long strands of hair, like a human's or a dwarf's but far coarser. Her steel knife couldn't hold enough of an edge to shave away the shameful strands no matter how carefully she worked the whetstone, so she used a piece of old tack she'd found in the barn to tie the strands into a lump in the back of her skull. During the Spanish-American War, her hands had been dexterous enough to work Lord Gatling's famous machine gun, but now her knuckles were the size of walnuts. She'd broken a tusk off short gnawing on a marrow-bone, and the roots of the rest of her teeth felt only tenuous. Her nose had grown weak, but not weak enough she didn't know she stank of something that wasn't quite mildew or decay or bad meat, a stench that could only be called *old orc*.

At least the barn had plenty of space to do the butchering, even with the giant heap of coal and the age-warped timbers wasting away and the open-top carriage that hadn't been used since before Mha's birth. Scattered barrels held scraps of wood and bits of iron and other detritus someone hadn't bothered to properly discard. Dusty shelves offered tools so corroded they imploded at a touch and mysterious half-full bottles. The six stalls hadn't seen beasts for ten years at least, but the stinks of hide and manure and horse-sweat had sunk into the dirt floor like wasted blood. Not that Mha would waste any of Uraz's blood.

The barn was for lost and useless things.

Like an orcess with no clan and no labor.

Like Uraz, Mha was naked. She didn't want to get his blood or grease on her clothes. The grooms' quarters had the tiny stove, but out here in the main barn, November's chill whistled between gaps in the plank walls, turning her breath to white plumes and raising bear pimples on her sagging skin.

Mha knotted the heavy hemp line around Uraz's ankles. She needed two tries to toss the line over the central beam, a mere fifteen feet up. Rusty saw blades in her spine and an even more agonizing brick in her throat, she hauled the line hand-over-hand to hoist her warrior's naked body so that his dangling hands hung inches above the floor. A double loop and quadruple half-hitch around one of the beams supporting the hayloft held him there.

Had the wind picked up? Did November approve of her efforts?

No, she couldn't think that. Orcish gods never gave. They only took. They commanded, never succored. She only thought she'd lost everything. If she dared protest to November or the Sun or Moon or even the sleeping soil, they would find something else to claim.

Watching Uraz's empty shell swing from his ankles, arms dangling almost to the hard-packed wooden floor, Mha fought for her own breath. It wasn't enough that her bent back cramped her lungs and the brick in her throat nearly choked her, the sight threatened to squeeze gasping *tears* from her. She knew every inch of his skin. That long twisted scar on the back of Uraz's ribs, where he'd had taken a sword blade meant for the human Lieutenant Harrison. The thick knot of scar where an overstrained rope had snapped, burning through his skin clear to the muscle. A lump where the first orc to try to claim their daughter Kiva had gouged a talon's width of meat away. And so many smaller scars, where she'd marked him each time they joyfully ravished each other. Though those lusts had died twenty years past, her memory held each scar as firmly as his flesh did.

8

Her warrior's body mapped their lives together.

Uraz had left her this final gift. She had not dishonored him by sobbing when she woke to find him cold. She had not cried when she'd undressed him, gently tracing each of his scars for one last time. She would not soil his memory by even hinting at ingratitude. Even if she was alone for the first time in forty years, even if the rocky lump in her throat swelled enough to wholly choke her, she would not cry.

An orc lived for their clan and their work. She had neither, but Mha would show the gods that taking everything but her breath would not break her. Like the warrior she had been.

When Uraz stopped swinging, she set the broad tin pan beneath him. As she'd hoped, it was exactly wide enough.

Now the worst part.

The first worst part.

Mha didn't dare hesitate. November would think her reluctant. She would not tolerate that.

So many orcs in America, not that she and Uraz had seen any in the last few summers, kept their talons indecently trimmed. How could an orc be an orc without talons? She set her thumb to the side of Uraz's neck. "Thank you for your final gift," she whispered. Not that Uraz would hear, but November would know that she honored her warrior.

She needed to be gentle. She didn't want to set Uraz swinging and disrespect his blood by splashing it across the dirt. She wanted to savor every bite of blood sausage.

Mha flicked her thumb against Uraz's still carotid.

Her talon hit hide—and cracked.

The pain in her thumb was minor, but the shock of breaking a talon on Uraz's hide wholly halted her breath. She stared at the cracked talon, heart thudding in her ears.

She'd cracked talons before, of course.

But age had taken even the power to truly claim her warrior.

Maybe her breath would never start again. Perhaps November would decide she had finally earned death.

But in another heartbeat, her treacherous ruin of a body demanded air.

She had to use the feeble knife to cut Uraz's throat. It wasn't sharp enough to cut him properly, but at least it wouldn't snap. She cradled the back of his head with one hand as she sawed, trying to keep the swaying to a minimum.

An awful minute later, thick red blood pinged into the tin pan.

Mha's vision blurred. How *dare* she? The barn seemed even colder than before—had November witnessed her shameful tear? She refused to raise a hand to wipe her eyes. If the tear had been seen, she had condemned herself. If it had not, she would not draw November's eye.

The barn's chill would slow his blood. He would be there for hours.

She couldn't put it off any longer.

If she could preserve Uraz's meat and tan his hide properly, so that his remains could succor her for as long as she lived, she could choose a proper final sacrifice for him. If she couldn't, if his whole body had to be consumed in a single feast or be wasted, she would have to sacrifice it all.

You couldn't smoke meat over a coal fire, so she'd have to salt-cure him. A lot of salt. The little box in the groom's quarters didn't come close.

If she found salt, she would tan Uraz's hide with his brains. If she couldn't make the necessary sacrifice, she'd surrender his hide with the rest of him.

If she found salt before she needed to eat or drink, her warrior could still shelter her against the world.

And in the pit of her heart, Mha so desperately wanted something of Uraz to stay.

That meant calling upon that most un-orcish of human customs.

A *favor*.

2

Stepping out of the dim barn into the clear morning, Mha blinked and raised an arm against the painful light. The winter-weakened Sun had dragged itself a quarter of the way across the sky, but November stole so much of its warmth the frost still gleamed across the vast grassy lawn. Drifts of dead leaves from the surrounding forest raised a stink of decay from their sheltered steaming innards, almost smearing the crisp cold air. November's wind slipped through gaps in the old horse blanket she'd stitched into the coat and cut straight through her canvas dress. She'd debated over the skulls of her three failed suitors, but decided to leave them on their shelf. Humans wouldn't understand the significance.

Her warrior hung in the barn behind her, turgid blood draining into a bucket before he froze, and the Sun shone as though the world hadn't ended. Maybe this year would be different. Maybe December Sun-Eater would fully devour the Sun. Plunge the world into a darkness as complete as that inside her.

December would not grant that fiercely held hope.

If she was to have anything at all, she must find salt.

Her only hope was the big white farmhouse at the far side of the meadow.

Frozen dirt crunched beneath her boots. The Army had issued her these misshapen boots when they'd claimed her labor for the Spanish-American War. Thirty years on, she'd worn the third set of soles so thin that only the cardboard liners kept the dirt out. If she could keep some of Uraz, she could make new boots. Proper, truly orcish boots.

Every other step sparked a flare of pain in her left hip. Each month, each week, that hip ached more. A slow-growing pain, demanding a hair's thickness more from her every day. Perhaps she needed to finally surrender to the humiliation of a staff? Using a staff while Uraz lived would have been an admission that she was too feeble to be worthy of him, but now…

She brushed the thought away. She would deal with Uraz's gift honorably. Making that last sacrifice, she would stand on her own feet. She could bear the pain one more day.

Nothing compared to the pain of relying on a *favor*.

Uraz and Mha had saved Lieutenant Harrison's life in the war. They had only done their duty as soldiers of the US Orc Army, but Harrison claimed a human sort of blood debt. Not a proper blood debt, where Harrison would serve the n'Tass clan all his days, but a human *favor* as feeble as a man's thighbone. The young human had fumbled trying to explain *favors* to a young Mha and Uraz, finally settling on *When you can't take, I will give.*

Senseless, senseless words behind a senseless human idea.

But *favor* had sheltered Mha and Uraz in Lieutenant Harrison's barn for these last three summers, even after the Lieutenant's death last summer. It had granted them the freedom of the woods, a heap of coal every month, oats and beans and bacon and a handful of salt or sugar or lard left at their door every week.

A feast of humiliation every day, for orcs who did nothing to earn it.

And now, Mha needed to invoke *favor* again.

A ten-pound bag of salt was nothing to a man. Perhaps Mha could do some service to earn it without the demeaning *favor*. The humans here didn't work the soil, or care for cows or horses, but surely they had some labor that would merit a bag of salt? Even age-twisted, she could carry a load that would cripple all but the biggest men.

Her finger caressed the knife-trimmed edge of the talon she'd broken against her warrior's neck, and wondered if that was still true.

A horseless carriage growled down the road beyond the line of trees at the front of the property. One of the new Model Ts, or Model As, or Model Another Stupid Meaningless Human Word. What was a T? Or an A? You couldn't point at a tree or a human or dirt or the Sun or even a despicable elf and say *This is a T*. More than one human had told her they were marks on paper, but that had to be a human prank. Why would you give marks on paper a name? You could make countless marks, of any sort you wanted, before using the paper to scrape your ass clean.

Perhaps the walk would shift the brick blocking Mha's guts.

It wasn't as painful as the brick in her throat, though.

Mha trudged past the human outhouse to the farmhouse's back door. The farmhouse was built so sturdily that it might have been intended for short orcs. The doorframe was timber, painted a shining white, and the door was solid planks of oak fit tightly together, sanded to be inseparable to human eyes, and stained a dark brown.

Mha had grown accustomed to the barn. The ceiling of the groom's quarters was so low, her awful *hair* brushed the plaster. The barn doors were comfortably tall. In the time since Uraz had brought them here, Mha had not once approached a building truly meant for humans.

The sight of this door added another layer of self-revulsion to her heart.

She had been strong. She had been tall. Her heart remembered being the sort of orcess that picked up a young recalcitrant cow under each arm before tossing them up onto the scale.

A normal human door should come up to her chin.

Her head could clear the farmhouse door without so much as a nod.

Heart shuddering anew, Mha's breath trembled in her lungs. Had age stolen so much from her? Was she so stooped? Her traitorous eyes threatened to erupt with tears again, so she squeezed them shut until they obeyed her.

If she'd worn her skulls, any orc that saw her would challenge her boast.

Humans wanted you to knock on their doors to request admission, then built doors that would fall off the hinges at the lightest touch. She rapped the back of her knuckles against the door, light as she could. The dim thud, inaudible even ten feet away, sent another shudder through her.

She was weak. Old and weak and useless.

Maybe once she'd cared for Uraz's gifts, the gods would let her die.

She knocked again, a little harder.

A muffled cry beyond the door answered. The humans knew she was present.

Mha made herself relax. She needed to be calm. Humans worried when an orc showed so much as a tusk, or breathed too deeply, or farted. Her sharp ears picked up the sound of slippered feet crossing a wooden floor, along with a peculiar double thump. Moments later, the door rattled and swung open.

The gaunt human wore a faded white house dress—*she*, the human had to be a she, only women wore dresses, even

18

though her skin hung so loose she might be sexless. She was even more bent than Mha, relying on a cane in each hand to keep her upright, head twisted almost cruelly forward so that she could see ahead. Wire-framed glasses with heavy lenses loomed on her beaklike nose, transforming her rheumy eyes into giant bloodshot orbs. She stank of grease and spearmint.

"Yes?" The woman started. "Oh, it's you!" She leaned on one cane to peer around Mha's flank. "It's usually your husband."

"Woman," Mha said formally. "I must invoke *favor*."

Before Mha could explain the woman said, "But of course!" She retreated a step, working her canes and legs in combination like a nightmare spider-horse. "Come in, come in! Wipe your feet, come in!"

What sort of human invited an orc into their home? Even in Mha's decrepitude, too bent to breathe well, one sneeze would shatter the old woman's spine. Human homes were full of breakable things spaced too closely together.

But Mha and Uraz were completely, un-orcishly dependent upon Lieutenant Harrison's *favor*.

Mha stepped inside and meticulously wiped the soles of her boots against the boar-bristle mat.

"Shut the door, shut the door," the woman said. "These old bones freeze too easy."

This had to be a kitchen. It had a coal stove, and a counter, and even one of the fancy iceboxes just like an Army mess hall. It didn't look anything like a mess hall, with smooth-plastered walls painted a pale blue and a pristine white ceiling. The smells of a dozen different dried spices and baking bread filled Mha's sinuses. A china cabinet displayed delicate white porcelain plates and tiny cups, all bearing identical intricate blue sketches that Mha's old eyes couldn't quite make out. An antique wooden claw-foot table dominated the room, surrounded by masterfully carved ladderback chairs that any of Mha's children would have broken with a hard look. The floor was so brightly polished that Mha could see the shape of her reflection, if not her features.

Mha had never smelled any place so weirdly clean.

The woman waved to a sturdy-looking bench. "Sit, sit. At our age, our bones need all the rest they can get. I was just putting water on for tea, it's no problem to add a little more."

Did *favor* require tea? Uraz drank tea each time he begged for food? What were *favor's* rules?

"Could you grab one of those big brown mugs off the top of the china cabinet before you sit?" the woman said, pouring water into a kettle. "I'm afraid it's a mite too heavy for these old bones."

The woman wanted her to go near the most breakable items in the kitchen? Was this a test? Did aged humans test orcs the way the Army had? And why would she keep a mug she couldn't reach and couldn't use? Keeping her steps as light as her treacherous hip permitted, Mha held her breath and plucked a mug down. It would hold perhaps a quart, and had a nearly orcish heft.

The woman set the kettle on the stove and tottered towards the table. "Sit, sit, my dear."

Mha sat. The bench was almost high enough to be comfortable.

"While that heats—oh, dear." The woman blinked. "I fear we've never been introduced, have we? And you, of course, are Mantis."

Humans! They couldn't speak an Orcish name properly if you stuffed them with apples and fennel and slow-roasted them over a hickory fire. "Mha-n'Tass." Maybe a little garlic. Garlic went well with man.

Ignoring her correction, the way humans always did, the woman turned a chair to face Mha and settled down. "My name is Rose, but everyone calls me Thorn. You must do so as well."

She had a name, but others refused to use it? Perhaps "Mantis" was as close a feeble human throat could get to her name, but "Thorn" sounded nothing like "Rose." How did humans stomach such disrespect?

Still, the woman had demanded a labor of using a wrong name. Mha would swallow the insult, so long as she didn't have the gall to ruin Uraz's name. Mha sucked her cold-chapped lips to moisten them. "Thorn."

"Just so!" the woman said. "What brings you out here, and not your fine orc husband?"

The knot in Mha's throat swelled until it threatened to burst. She didn't dare shout past it. Such words demanded to be shouted, but shouting would scare Thorn and might make her summon the police. "My warrior is dead."

The woman leaned back. "Oh, you poor thing! I am so sorry. How can I help you? Do you need help with arrangements? Should I send word to someone?"

Mha's heart pounded. This tiny birdlike woman, intruding on Uraz's final gift? Her hands twitched with the instinct to leap across the room and swipe her talons across the old lady's throat. The urge lacked heat, though. Mha's old blood didn't boil the way it once had. And could her talons pierce even human hide any longer?

"No," Mha said. "I need salt."

Thorn raised a hand to her mouth. "Orcs bury their dead with salt? I had no idea! Bristol would never talk of his time serving with orcs, you know. Except for the part where you and your husband saved his life." She leaned closer and reached out a hand, almost as if she wanted to touch Mha. Which was silly. Humans didn't touch orcs if they could avoid it. "You gave me another twenty-nine years with the man I love. You don't have to worry. The barn is yours as long as you live. It's in my will."

What did Thorn's willpower have to do with the barn? Mha was sixty years old, and still understood nothing of humans. "It was duty."

23

"Now don't discount yourself!" Thorn lightly slapped both her knees. "Your man shoved Bristol out of the way and took a bayonet meant for him. The fall popped his knee, so you carried him away to safety before he got trampled. I know the whole story, see?" One side of her mouth cricked upwards. "By the time he healed up, the war was over. You were sent by God to keep my man safe, and I won't forget it. Whatever you need that I can give you, is yours."

Mha needed worthwhile labor. She needed a hip that didn't pain and hands without giant swollen knuckles and a back so bent that she could walk through a human door. She needed the hair to fall away, restoring her beautiful green-purple scalp.

Thorn's offer meant nothing.

And sent by God? Human gods did not even notice orcs.

On the coal stove, the warming kettle hissed and spat.

"I can work," Mha said. "For salt."

"Oh don't be silly!" Thorn said. "How much do you want?"

Silly? Mha's pulse throbbed in her vision. How was

offering labor for salt silly? No, she couldn't let human strangeness distract her. The best way to deal with humans was to ignore the senseless things, swallow the insults, and say what you needed. "Ten pounds. I can move firewood. Or rocks."

"Nonsense." Thorn waved her hand. "In the pantry. Let's take a look."

Would she refuse labor? Did humans count *favor* so strongly?

Mha set the mug on the bench and followed.

In the Army, a pantry was a food warehouse. Thorn's pantry was the same, on a smaller scale. Big enough for Mha and Thorn to stand side by side, with wooden shelves lining the walls and tiny cans and boxes and jars lining the shelves. Sacks of flour and sugar and rice filled the floor space beneath the shelves. Mha had never imagined one person having so much food, so many different kinds of food. She recognized the beans and the red goop of tomatoes. But what were the jars of yellow orbs suspended in dark liquid standing in precise rows, ready for inspection whenever the Lieutenant returned? Were those peaches?

Humans could have peaches all year long? Mha's mouth watered at the thought.

"My nephew, the ungrateful wretch, comes by every weekend to make sure I have everything I need and to do a few chores," Thorn said. "He brings me more than I can possibly eat. He *says* it's because he's afraid I'll get snowed in, but I'm sure it's just because he doesn't want to drive all the way out to Clinton Township when the weather's bad." Her head turned as she studied the bags and boxes. "He thinks I should move down to Detroit near him, like I would ever leave the home Bristol made for us. My son thinks I should move out to New York City with him, where he's got his fancy bank job. He's a vice-president, you know. He had the phone put in and everything." Her cane thrust out. "There. That little cask. That's the salt, left over from last year's canning. Here, let me out and you can pick it up."

The cask was big enough for twenty pounds of salt. How full was it? Mha's hope thrummed. She tried to dampen it before November noticed and was compelled to thwart it. She made herself watch Thorn's two-cane shamble back to her seat, refusing to surrender to dangerous hope.

"Go on, then," Thorn said. "Pick it up. I'll make the tea."

Mha lifted the keg's loose lid.

It was nearly full.

If Thorn permitted her the whole cask, Mha could accept every scrap of Uraz's final gift. Not just the meat, but the organs and bowels as well.

Mha commanded her heart to slow. "I could move coal for this,"

"Oh, you go on," Thorn said. "Take it, take it. You more than earned a few pounds of salt."

Earned? How had Mha *earned* this?

No, she couldn't get angry. She'd already lost her pride by living too long.

The cask felt far heavier than twenty pounds.

Thorn said, "I have a jar in the cupboard I use for cooking. When Pete shows up this weekend, I'll send him tooty-sweetie for another box."

Escaping the pantry had its own challenge. If she turned around, her back side would probably bump the canned peaches, or maybe the bag of flour. Or the sugar—how did

27

humans stomach that awful stuff? Mha backed up, each unnatural step triggering an unfamiliar ache in her rotting hip, glancing left and right before each motion to be sure she wouldn't accidentally knock down a wall.

Not that she could wreck a human's house. Not anymore. Not like when she was young and worthwhile.

She emerged to find Thorn had set a china cup and the mug on the table, and was pouring hot water into a teapot barely bigger than the mug. "Set that by the door and have a sit. I still have some cookies left from yesterday's baking. And prunes, but you don't want them. Nobody wants them, but I get stopped up something fierce and nothing clears you like a prune. It happens to old ladies like us."

Thorn thought she was like Mha? An orc was nothing like a human!

But…

They were both old.

Both lived alone.

They'd borne their children. Those children had gone away.

Like Mha, nobody remained to eat Thorn.

"Sit a spell," Thorn said.

Mha shoved her disquieting thoughts away. Even if she wanted to eat with a human, she could neither eat nor drink until she made Uraz's final sacrifice. "Uraz-n'Tass needs me."

Thorn's entire face drooped. Was she disappointed? "Of course, of course. It's selfish of me." She set the kettle back on the stove. "Listen. It's just us ladies now. We can't be all formal. If you get lonesome, you just come up and knock on that door. We'll have tea and chat, and you can tell me what you need my nephew to bring for you. I'm sure you get tired of oats and lard, don't you?"

Get lonesome? Mha's entire life would be lonesome. Uraz had nuzzled her neck before sleeping last night. That would be the last true contact she would have in all her days, and she would treasure that memory in the pit of her heart as long as she lived.

And when she died, she'd rot until she was found.

Chatting with a human would shorten her days when her heart burst from frustration.

And what sort of human would welcome Mha to her fragile dainty kitchen?

3

November had stripped away the forest's greenery, leaving an impassible tangle of vines and low-hanging branches on all sides. Every time the breeze surged, it carried scents of burning leaves and distant coal and November's constant decay. Leaves crunched beneath her bare feet as she trudged down the path, a knot of bloody gristle in each hand. The knot in her throat had not eased, but thirst had added its burn.

Make sacrifice, then she could drink. Eat a scoop of leftover porridge. Spend half an hour in the outshed Uraz had built behind the barn, heaving at the brick in her guts. Begin cutting and salting and tanning.

And dress.

An orc's final sacrifice must be made naked. Anything she wore, anything she carried, the gods would strip from her like the scudding clouds stripped the Sun's warmth from her skin. Mha kept her thoughts as empty as she could. Her greatest treasure were memories of Uraz. She would not offer any more of those than she must.

A few minutes hobbling through the woods brought her to the clearing she and Uraz had chosen. Wide enough for a dozen orcs to brawl, with long brown grass that cracked and crackled at each step, just like her bones. The ankle-deep stream still flowed freely, but its mocking laughter sounded cold.

The Sun was almost at its highest point when she reached the rock. She and Uraz had sat on it yesterday on their daily walk through the woods. They had stopped here more and more often, Uraz saying he would share the Sun's gift of light with his woman. She had thanked him, refusing to shame him by noticing his shallow breath.

Even when Uraz could no longer claim her body, he claimed her heart every day.

Her warrior had fought for her until the end.

She knelt before the rock.

Sobs threatened to come ripping straight up from her and out her face, spilling scornful tears and broken breath. Swallowing them was even harder than cutting Uraz's throat, harder still than choosing what to sacrifice.

Mha opened her hands.

In the left, Uraz's heart.

In the right, his privates.

The blood hadn't finished draining, but they were still pale and shrunken.

The cuts should be smooth, like orcish talons. Not brutally hacked from his flesh by a knife more saw than blade.

Mha took a deep breath. She must say this clearly. She must not be misunderstood.

When she thought she could speak, she raised her face and stared at the Sun. "Sun! Light of day. I thank you for Uraz's life. He fought for me all his days."

Her throat tightened again, her guts clenching around the brick of turd.

The Moon was not visible, but it would hear. The Moon knew everything. "Moon! Keeper of secrets! I thank you for Uraz's nights. He brought me pleasure in every one!" The pleasure had faded, but as she aged she'd found warmth alone a milder pleasure.

Her next breath was brazenly ragged, a disgrace. Her chest refused her commands, so she pushed her air out as hard as she could, hoping that volume could make up for shakiness. "November! My Uraz sought death all his days. I thank you for granting it to him."

She should be surrounded by the clan. Even if orcs born in America would not end their elders, would not take those final gifts, she should at least be surrounded by sons and their wives and their babes. She should be living with her own blood, not left alone in a barn in the wilderness with a strange human woman who would offer her *tea.*

No. No distractions. Complete the sacrifice.

Mha bowed her head to stare at the rock. The heart that had driven the passion of his spirit, the privates that had driven the passion of his flesh. Two pathetic shriveled offerings, left on cold stone.

More of an offering than she would leave of herself.

She could barely force the words out. "I thank you for my love. My warrior. My Uraz."

There. She'd left his name for the gods. She would never speak it again.

Bitterness overwhelmed her. She had lived her whole life as an orc ought. And she would end her days here, without a warrior? Without useful labor? With no reason, no purpose? The gods took everything from an orc, but couldn't they at least grant her death in return? Why couldn't someone, anyone, just eat her?

The Sun peered around a cloud.

Mha's breath caught.

She'd knelt at her warrior's last sacrifice, and dared to demand?

November had certainly witnessed her. Had the Sun seen as well?

It didn't matter. There was nothing November or the Sun could take from her. If either claimed the barn she called home, December the Sun-Eater would freeze her blood to her bone.

And she would welcome it.

Stifling the groan, she rose to her feet and walked from the clearing without looking back, leaving her warrior's shriveled heart and orchood and name behind. When she returned, if she ever returned, they would all be gone.

The wind gnawed at her bare skin, sucking away what little warmth she still held. She refused to let it speed her step. An orc endured, even when the wind tried to make her skin as cold as her heart.

She'd left her coat and dress by the outshed her warrior had built. Before pulling them on, she dipped water from the rain barrel and washed the heart's blood from her hands and empty breasts. Five orcs had suckled at them. Another had once admired them. Now, as useless as the rest of her and even more annoying, the way they flopped around.

It was done.

And he would still nurture her. A bite of meat, every day. New boots. A leather dress. Bits and drabs of her warrior, to shelter her and warm her and protect her.

Mha was reaching for the barn door when she heard the soft cry.

Between the human outhouse and the farmhouse, a figure in white flailed at the ground.

Grateful for any distraction, Mha stomped towards the farmhouse.

Thorn had fallen, arms and legs and canes flying every which way. The woman sucked in breaths bigger than a tiny human should be able to hold. One hand still held a cane.

The other cane lay well out of her reach. Eyes watering and blinking, she stared up at Mha. "I seem to have fallen."

Humans, explaining the obvious, would never stop annoying Mha. But she needed to think of something else, anything else, other than her warrior and the gut-wrenching task that would fill the next few days. "Are you hurt?"

Thorn raised her hands and flexed her legs. "I don't think so. My other cane is missing, though. Can you see it?"

Mha knelt to pick it up.

"It's my own fault," Thorn babbled. "It's the prunes, you see. They help when things stop, but when they start again I get in such a rush and the grass was still icy underneath. I can't abide the old chamber pots."

Mha offered her the cane.

Thorn said, "Could you offer a hand?"

Mha had helped wounded human soldiers to their feet before, helping them get upright so they could keep a little self-respect by hobbling off the battlefield. Thorn's tiny hand felt like helping a butterfly aloft.

"Thank you, my dear," Thorn said.

Did the woman think Mha roamed the woods eating grasses?

36

Getting her canes braced beneath her, Thorn said, "If you'd care to come back in half an hour or so, or any time, we could have that tea. Just knock on the door."

Why did she persist in that offer? Was Thorn so lonesome she would take an orc as company? The only thing Mha could think to do was offer the human parting respect chant and walk away. "Thank you, human."

"Do call me Thorn, I said."

Mha nodded. "Thorn. Thank you, Thorn."

Halfway back to the barn, Mha stopped.

She had knelt at Ur—at her warrior's final sacrifice, heart overflowing with bitterness at not having her clan or labor or her warrior.

November and the Sun *had* heard her.

And answered.

An old, decaying, worthless orcess wanted labor? Then let her help an equally rotting humaness. She'd thought the gods could take nothing more. They had taken the dare, and followed it by claiming her dignity, her patience, her peace of mind.

Mha ached to bellow reproach at the Sun itself.

But if she did, the gods would find something else to take. She couldn't imagine what remained, but they would find it.

Instead, she trudged back to the barn, fragrant with long-dead horses and the coppery stench of her warrior's still-draining blood. November's chill would help preserve his blood and meat.

She found her boots. Sat on the chunk of tree stump she used as a stool. Tried to ignore the aches in her heart and her throat, and the more concrete pain in her gut. And thought.

She must have a reason. An orc could not pound on a human's door without a reason.

Some time later, the outhouse door slammed on its spring. In another dozen breaths, the farmhouse door shut. Thorn was back in her home.

Mha steadied her breath. Hoisted herself to her feet. Perhaps she should carve a cane from her warrior's thigh bones? That would allow him to support her even more. No, that was for later. For now, she would obey the commands of season and Sun.

Heart pounding and November wind at her back, she trudged across the yard and knocked on the door, as instructed.

When Thorn's delighted face appeared Mha said, "Tell me of these *prunes*."